I0682505

Selfless

M. Anthony

3G Publishing, Inc.
Loganville, Ga 30052
www.3gpublishinginc.com
Phone: 1-888-442-9637

©2015 M. Anthony. All rights reserved.

No part of this book may be reproduced, stored in a retrieval system, or transmitted by any means without the written permission of the author.

First published by 3G Publishing, Inc. November, 2015.

ISBN: 9781941247204

Printed in the United States of America

Because of the dynamic nature of the Internet, any web addresses or links contained in this book may have changed since publication and may no longer be valid. The views expressed in this work are solely those of the author and do not necessarily reflect the views of the publisher, and the publisher hereby disclaims any responsibility for them.

Contents

Chapter One   5
Life is Good, Real Good

Chapter Two   13
Red-Eye, Green Eyes

Chapter Three   19
Uncle O'Neal

Chapter Four   29
Unconditional Love

Chapter Five   43
The Best Little Whorehouse in Atlanta

Chapter Six   49
Wild Horses

Chapter Seven   53
All Man

Chapter Eight   61
No Words

Chapter Nine   *79*
Alive Man Walking

Chapter Ten   *83*
Don't Judge A Book By Its Cover

Chapter Eleven   *95*
Where Life Ends, it Begins

Chapter Twelve   *111*
Is This Love

Chapter Thirteen   *125*
Selfishly Selfless

Chapter One

Life is Good, Real Good

Arielle, steps into the private elevator and pushes the penthouse button to his apartment. She leans back and smiles, then adjusts her tight, expensive skirt and blouse. She reaches into her purse and pulls out a compact mirror and checks her lipstick, hair and makeup… she's flawless and she knows it. 30 looks good, really good on her because she doesn't look a day over 25. Her strong, Latino genes are serving her well with glowing honey skin and the perfect hourglass figure that leave men contemplating, ruminating a life change just to be with her…and that's at first glance. But Arielle is not that woman, not that girl. She is tall, sophisticated, smart and business savvy. Her multiple degrees don't even touch the surface of all that she is capable of. Her style and grace demands attention when she is present, but her genuine goodness and virtue puts you at ease. Her beauty stands out, no doubt, but her meek, kind disposition is what really makes her special. By no means is she privileged and her roots keep her humble, always grateful for another day. This is no ordinary woman and she lives no ordinary life.

The elevator door opens to an upscale high-rise loft apartment. Arielle steps off the elevator slowly, one Louboutin at a time, into the very plush apartment. Expensive artwork covers the walls as she enters the living room area. No one is there. She looks toward the kitchen area and it's empty. Sitting her purse on the leather couch, she adores a fresh bouquet of peach and yellow roses on the French marble console. It is obvious she feels at home. A few moments later she heads into a bedroom and there's no one there. She walks back out and sheepishly steps around the corner from the kitchen and looks at the basketball court, but no one is there either, so she slowly walks to the master bathroom, opens the door and glances toward the shower. Another smile escapes as she admires a man with his back turned to her, standing 6'2", 210 pounds of well-chiseled, in a soft, yet Mandingo-like warrior skin tone. His name is Michael. Arielle , aroused and anxious starts to undress herself. She takes off her shirt slowly, one button at a time, then effortlessly sliding it off her shoulders. The blouse drops to the floor, exposing her beautiful perked, flawless supple breasts with 1/2 inch nipples at attention. Then she quickly releases her skirt and in one motion, pushes it to the floor, along with her panties. She steps out of the skirt, opening her legs just enough to expose her freshly groomed vagina. Her heart starts to beat faster, not in a ravenous way, but more of a tender embrace. And now she is standing there, gazing upon his body from head to toe, even though she herself would be considered a sex goddess, undeniably God's gift to man.

"Uhh Ehmm!"

She clears her throat to get Michael's attention. He turns around quickly and his surprise becomes a smile.

"Arielle , how long have you been standing there?"

"Not long," she replies as he opens the shower door for her. Michael looks intently as she places her hands on his chest. The dance begins. Water starts to runs down the side of her face, wetting her hair. Michael caresses her face with both hands, kisses her forehead, then her lips and down to her neck. By this time, Arielle has both her hands on his 9 inch cock, squeezing and stroking it in tune with him caressing her breasts. He then sits on the stone shower bench as she straddles him. As the light from the crystal and gold chandelier reflect on their glistening bodies Michael began licking and sucking her breasts. And in one motion without using her hands, she sat down on his cock until it disappeared inside of her. Their eyes closed and the dance continued as they disappeared behind a billowing mass of steam. After 30 minutes or so, it carries over into the bed. They made love until they were both exhausted and fell asleep in each other's arms.

Michael's alarm goes off at 6:00am and after turning it off he then turned back to that dreaded empty side of the bed. This was a familiar moment that made him feel some type of way. Reluctantly, he reached under the pillow and pulled out a lavender colored envelope and stared at it for a moment. Moments later, he leaned over, opened the bottom drawer of the nightstand and discarded the envelope among the sea of endless lavender envelopes, and shut the drawer.

Michael is driving down the freeway in his CL 63 Mercedes Benz Coupe listening to Isaac Hayes. Life is good and he feels good. As he settles into his monogrammed leather and mink seats, he thinks of his family and Arielle . He has come a long way from being an orphan with his little brother. Educated and well-traveled, he lives good, eats good, takes care of his family and friends and handles his businesses well. His humble beginnings and pain cause him not to brag, but deep down inside he is thankful and proud of his accomplishments. He pulls up to the health club he owns, and is greeted in the parking lot by Amy, who manages the club. Amy is a tall, beautiful, 23 year old black female with a body like an Olympic sprinter ..

"Good morning," Amy says with a twinkle in her eye. "What are you doing here so early?"

"I just came in to help you open up today."
Michael grabs his gym bag and juice mug out
of the car and walks past Amy, who gives him
a look over from head to toe. His physique
never ceases to amaze her.

"Well, I can surely use the help."

They go inside to open up the health club
for the day. 9 o'clock rolls around and Amy
enters Michael's office. He's sitting at his desk
doing paperwork when she walks over waiting
to be acknowledged. Michael looks up and
pushes away from his desk. Then, Amy sits on
his desk and straddles him by putting her feet
on both sides of the chair. Without saying a
word, she just stares at him with enticing eyes.
Michael, unmoved, sits back.

"Amy, what are you doing?"

Amy leans in.

"You know you want some of this sweet
pussy."

Michael smiles, in that I would love to but
kind of way. He knows this can't happen. Amy,
although beautiful and very attractive, is like
family. Michael has always taken pride in his
"big brother" and mentor role in her life. He

would never jeopardize that relationship…and he would never take advantage of her. Amy is a strong young woman and like any other young, impressionable woman her age, she can make some very different choices. But Michael loves and respects her enough to never, ever cross that line.

"Amy you know I love you like a little sister." Amy eases up a little, then leans back in.

"Yeah but I'm not that 17 year old little girl you first met."

And she's not. Amy has known Michael for quite some time now. She has always admired his character, his compassion and obviously his good looks. She was also grateful for is help over the years, taking care of her emotionally, supporting her financially and paying for her education. What started out as a loving, tender, sibling bond-like affection has recently grown into a healthy, male figure attraction…and he knows he must tread lightly.

"Trust me, I see you, and you're definitely a beautiful and sexy grown woman, but you will always be like a little sister to me."

Michael gently rest his hand on Amy's face as he stands up and plants a kiss on her forehead. Amy takes a deep breath and smiles. She loves Michael to death, but she knows in her heart that he is right. It would be nice to have him as her man, but she respects the kind of love he has for her, even though it attracts her even more. Michael quickly moves on.

"And why are you in here bothering me anyway?"

Recognizing his move, a hopelessly-in-some-kind-of-love Amy resumes employee mode. She willingly accepts this defeat.

"Well I thought you could teach the first aerobics class for me so I can get caught up on some paperwork. I need to get out of here on time tonight."

Michael is relieved and agrees.

"Sure I got you. Just give me five minutes, so I can finish up here."

Chapter Two

Red-Eye, Green Eyes

Michael is in the car headed to the airport to catch a late afternoon flight out to New Orleans, Louisiana. While he enjoys the scenery and his jazz music, he can't help but smile and think about his amusing encounter with Amy that morning. It made him feel uncomfortable, but he was flattered to say the least. The more he thought about it, he had noticed a few hints, but wasn't really sure and just hoped he was wrong, doing his best to dismiss the notion that she would ever come on to him. He was just glad that he was quick and gentle enough to diffuse the situation with no major bruising to anyone's ego.

After arriving at the airport, Michael parks his car, and makes his way to his boarding area. As he walks through the terminal, of course all eyes were on him. Michael's presence, his aura simply demanded attention. He cleaned up very well and today was no different. Italian suit jacket, expensive jeans, one of a kind shoes ....oh, and the Louis Vuitton man-bag to match. Michael was confident and rarely gave attention to his audience. Don't get it wrong, he was humble and genuinely a good person, but he never acted as if he was above anyone or anything. He was blessed and very fortunate to live his life and he didn't take that for granted, at all.

Finally seated, Michael checks his phone for last minute messages. He is approached in first class by two smitten flight attendants. They asked how long he was going to be in New Orleans.

"I'm only in town for one day."

One of the flight attendants gave him her cell number and said if he "was looking for a good time to just give them a call and that they would make it worth his while." Apparently they had a three day layover and were not shy with their invitation. Michael, who was very familiar with this approach accepted the number and with a smile replied "I'll be sure to get at you."

Michael's plane lands, he grabs his bag from overhead and made his way out to curb side, where he was picked up by a limousine, supplied with a bottle of champagne and a box of his favorite DeLafée gold chocolate truffles. This was a great start to his evening. Twenty-five minutes go by and the limo pulls into the grandiose driveway of a huge Louisiana style home. Michael gets out and walks to the front door and before he can ring the doorbell, the door opens, revealing a beautiful 5"11 green eyed Creole woman, with a very small waist and welcoming beautiful, bare size C breasts, nipples at attention, dressed only in a pair of purple panties. Michael stops for a moment and takes it all in a few seconds. He enjoyed the view and he wanted her to know.

Her name is Lucinda, who just happens to be one of the richest women in the state of Louisiana. She is literally fire. She lives the best, works the best and plays the best. Michael was quite fond of her and enjoyed her company. He respected her grind and her status, most importantly her "boss-bitch" attitude which keeps her at the top of her business game. Gotta love a woman who's rich and a boss, not to mention insanely sexy for 55. They kiss passionately, and Michael picks her up and carries her up a long flight of stairs into a massive and luxurious master bedroom. He gently lays her on the bed while sliding his hand under her arm and up her back, until her head is rests in the palm of his hand. He is lying on top of her with one thigh between her legs and staring into those big beautiful eyes with a mere inch between their faces. They are so close that he can feel her breath on his face. After a few moments of breathing her breath, he can now feel her vagina throbbing against his thigh, and softly kisses her lips. He then moves down to her neck and kisses it. She is fighting total surrender of her body. He kisses the center of her chest and lingers there for a while, going from breast to breast, kissing, sucking and licking. He then gently licks her stomach as he off her panties, then slowly spreading her legs. Lucinda is losing her battle. She is moaning, squirming, releasing her will in anticipation of what's to come. Michael puts his head between her legs and immediately begins to tease her vagina, with an occasional lick causing her legs to tighten up on the sides of his face. He continues to lick and suck and lick and suck for the next twenty minutes or so while she is screaming out in passion. Then, all of a sudden he stops and raises up to his knees as he watches her with a smile on his face. She trembles and shakes and trembles and shakes. She knows he is amused and she barely utters, "Don't laugh at me," in between quivers. Suddenly, he reaches over and puts his arms in the bends of her legs and jerks her to the edge of the bed in a very aggressive way. With no hands, he shoves his penis inside her vagina over and over, harder and deeper repeatedly for several minutes. Her screams get louder and louder!

"Fuck me! Fuck me harder! Fuck me!"

And he does. Just before he comes, he pulls out and forcefully turns her over to where her feet are on the floor and she is bending over on the bed. He then penetrates her from behind and starts to pound her vagina so hard, over and over until she screams out "STOP, STOP,

STOP!" And it is only when she begins to cry that he comes and then stops.

Breathing hard, with what life she has left, she climbs up on the bed and gently collapses. Michael lays next to her, waiting for her to fall asleep. As he rests his eyes for a moment, it doesn't take long for her to slip into a deep, satisfying sleep. He takes one last, long look at her and quietly gets up and heads to the shower. Once dressed, he summons the limo driver and heads back to the airport to catch his red-eye flight back to Atlanta.

Chapter Three

Uncle O'Neal

The high-pitched siren sound blares through the room. Dismissing the alarm on his phone, he sees there are two voicemails. The first is from his brother, Brandon, who is 4 years younger than Michael and married with two children. Michael adores his four year old nephew Cameron and two year old niece Brielle. He never imagined he could love two kids the way he does, but he would die for them. He often thought about what it would be like to have his own...especially with her. He knew he wanted a family one day, but everything had to be perfect.

"Hey, bro. Chanel and the kids would like to see you, so why don't we meet at the restaurant for dinner? Call me if tonight is good. Love you, Bro."

The next beep comes through and it's from Francisco, Michael's longtime friend of nine years and his accountant. He is loyal and means the world to Michael. It was unfortunate that a hunting accident, 11 years ago left him paralyzed from the waist down. Michael took great pride in being his friend, his confidante and watched over him like a brother. He owed him that much and more.

"Hey, Michael. I need to go over some figures with you from the restaurant, so drop by tomorrow morning if you can. Hit me back." Michael sits up and texts him back "See you at 9:00 in the morning." Then, he texts Brandon, "I'll be at the restaurant at 6pm and miss you guys, too."

The day has been long and Michael has fulfilled his usual routine of errands and meetings. Nothing can quite make his day complete than spending time with his family. They were close and it was the most important thing in his life. And next in line was his businesses including the restaurant he was headed to. Family dinner was everything and more. Michael loved to relax and unwind and be himself completely…it was always a "no flex" zone. Although he owns several businesses which have served him very well over the years, he was grateful, yet very proud to be able to live comfortably, charitably and take care of his family.

As he approaches the back parking lot of the restaurant it seems like all hell is breaking loose. Michael quickly exits his car, slamming the door and rushes over to his brother, Brandon, who is standing in the middle of Uncle O'Neal and Tim, who is the restaurant manager and Michael's childhood friend. Tim, a handsome, openly gay man is screaming at Uncle O'Neal while Brandon is holding them apart.

"What the hell is going on here?" Michael shouts, staring down both men. Everyone takes a pause, but not for long. Tim is the first to speak….."Michael, I am so fed up with him coming in my kitchen looking and smelling like that. He's contaminating my kitchen. He won't even wash his hands and I'm sick of it."

All eyes reluctantly went to Uncle O'Neal, Michael and Brandon's favorite uncle. He was tall, dark and his Rambo-like physique coupled with his hard looks often threw people off. But Uncle O'Neal who is a homeless, ex-war veteran, was actually harmless. Michael took a deep breath.

"Uncle O you know better, and we have had this conversation before."

Uncle O just drops his head, turns and walks away. Yes, he knew that was truth, but it still felt bad coming from Michael. Brandon caught up with him.

"Uncle O wait up."

Michael and Tim went inside and headed to the office. Brandon and Uncle O are walking off, side by side and Brandon asks,

"Uncle O, what were you thinking? You know how particular Tim is when it comes to his kitchen."

Uncle O, slows up a bit and finally looks forward. He loves Brandon and decides to ease up before responding.

"You know I love that old punk, and I would die for him, but he better learn to respect me or I'll whoop his ass."

Brandon smiles, he gets it. Uncle O is old school and all he wants is respect. It doesn't matter that he is homeless, or may smell or even appears disheveled at times…he just required respect. It was obvious he had some issues, but he was a good man and he always looked out for Michael and Brandon, the kids and even Tim. They were his family. - His feelings were sometimes hurt by even the slightest reprimand, so Brandon always appealed to his sense of family, which he knew meant the world to him. He suffered from anxiety, mainly PTSD, but he always did what was right and protected those he loved. His "boys" understood him and accepted all of him.

"Uncle O, do you know that when Aunt Sharon was raising us after our mother and father passed, she was stealing our inheritance and would never buy us any nice things… Tim would sneak and give Michael his clothes and shoes until you came and took us to live with Mrs. Doris? Tim has always been like a brother to us. And, Uncle O don't you think it's time for you to come off the streets? You know Mom and Dad's house is there for you and it's got everything you need. All you have to do is pay the utilities. Michael, Tim, and I are so tired of worrying about you being out here on these streets."

Uncle O sighed. He hated pity and he hated when they worried.

"You guys don't have to worry about me. Y'all know that the war fucked my head up, but living inside would sure enough kill me. I need to sleep outside or I can't breathe. I know you guys love me, and if I never tell you again, you and your brother are all I got. I will give my life for y'all at anytime. If I could have died in that car crash instead of your mom and dad I would have. Your father is the only reason I'm alive today. I love you and your brother with all my heart, with everything"

Brandon, feeling the love in his words, put his hand on Uncle O'Neal's shoulder.

"We know Uncle O. We know."

They embrace one another with a long hug. This is family and all they have are each other. Even though Uncle O was not a biological uncle, he was their late father's best friend and he treated them like they were his sons. They were indebted to him for all his support and the love he showed even to this day, despite his shortcomings. All of a sudden, Uncle O'Neal jumped back!

"Oh Shit! Brandon if you really want to help me, I forgot to tell you I just killed a mother-fucker, and I need to get out of the country." Brandon was shook and puzzled...what did he do now?

"What the fuck Uncle O!" What do you need? What can I do?

Uncle O'Neal, looked from side-to-side before anxiously leaning in. Brandon cautiously looks around too.

"Yeah, I need to get out of the country, loan me five dollars."

Brandon paused and smiled as he shook his head. He should have known.

"Uncle O you crazy. Hey, Chanel and the kids are inside. They would love to see you."

Uncle O, smiled and they both chuckled.

"Okay, let's go see those little bad children of yours."

They walked back up to the restaurant. Michael is in the office trying to calm Tim down Tim is so frustrated and barely lets Michael get a word in.

"Michael, I am so sick of him coming in my kitchen when he won't even wash his hands. I try and make sure he always has food. I even drive around some days and find him, just to make sure he's eating."

Michael knows the situation and he knows that Tim has a right to be upset.

"Tim you don't have to explain yourself to me. I know you care and go out of your way for him, and for that he and I both love you man...But Tim, I never told you the whole story of how Uncle O came into our lives. O is really not my uncle. He was my dad's best friend. They grew up together. They went into the Marines together to try and have a better life, but Uncle O couldn't handle it. My dad saved his life in there and looked after him the entire time they were in the Marines. Uncle O almost lost his mind. But when mom and dad died and my mom's sister moved in with us as our guardian, only to steal all our inheritance, it was Uncle O that removed us from that bad situation. He took us to live with Cheryl and Mrs. Doris when Brandon was eight and I was twelve. Then, when I turned eighteen, it was Uncle O that helped me get my parent's home back from Aunt Doris. He practically saved us…from God knows what could have happened!"

A nullified Tim, breathes with frustration, but relents somewhat because he knows most of what Uncle O has done and he pretty much has love for him too.

"Yea, but he did take you to live in a whore house disguised as a boarding house.

Michael smiles and unapologetically responds.

"And it was one of the best things that could've ever happened to us, and that's why I love him".

"Say no more," said Tim.

Michael walks out of the office, through the kitchen and out into the restaurant. As he's making his way over to the VIP section -to have dinner with his family, he hears Ripley, the beautiful and talented house entertainer

"Ladies, do you see that fine specimen of a man easing across the dining room headed toward the VIP section? That luscious hunk of chocolate is the owner of this fine establishment, and his name is Michael. Look at him. Don't you just want to take a bite out of him?"

And the house applauds. Michael shakes his head and smiles as he makes his way over to his family. The kids are too happy to see their favorite uncle and they overwhelm him with laughter, playful hugs and punches. Michael manages to hug his sister-in-law Chanel, then puts Cameron and Brielle in his lap. Brandon and Uncle O are already tearing up the appetizers and laughing about old times. This is it, what Michael lives for. They enjoyed dinner and the evening together, safe, sound and as a family.

Chapter Four

Unconditional Love

Michael hits the alarm… its 6:45am already. He sits up in bed and takes a look at all of his appointments for the day. Suddenly he gets an alert for his 9 am meeting with Francisco. He turns to get out of bed, but not before gazing at the bottom drawer. He leans over and opens it just enough to see a glimpse of lavender, then shuts it. He closes his eyes and takes a deep breath and heads for the shower.

Michael steps off the elevator and takes a few steps and adjusts his Rolex, when he gets another alert that his next appointment is in 30 mins. He makes his way down to the parking garage where he is confronted by D.J, a six year old, one man wrecking crew. It appears to Michael that D.J. has written all over his Porsche.

"Hey, what are you doing D.J.?"

D.J. quickly turns around with one hand behind his back, as he postures himself accordingly.

"What it look like Big Man? It seem like you have a problem that only I can fix".

D.J. points to the marked car. Michael is once again amused and plays along as usual. He gets a kick out of this little, wanna-be menace to society.

"Oh yea, what's that?"

D.J. is excited but tries to stay in big boy business mode.

"Well, if you want me to catch and stop whoever is writing all over your car, it's going to cost you ten dollars a year and I'll make your problem go away." Michael pretends to ponder the idea and puts on a straight face.

"Well alrighty then, why don't I just give you twenty dollars a month to look after all the cars down here?"

D.J. is surprised and his eyes light up…but he catches himself and frowns a little before responding.

"Let me talk to my sister first, to see if that's a good deal, and I'll get back to you Michael extends his hand out for a man-shake.

"Cool, but if you take this deal and something else happens to these cars, I will find the culprit and break him in two. Do you hear me?"

DJ smiles. "Yes big man, I hear you well!"

"Ok good, now take your sleeve and wipe that crayon off my car!"

D.J. starts to wipe frantically. Still excited about the $20 job offer.

"Ok, ok, calm down big man. I'll get it."

Michael laughs and proceeds to walk around his car, inspecting for more art. He has known DJ a few years now and he knows he is a good kid. He is also very smart for his age and attends one of the most prestigious schools for gifted children in the area. DJ and his older sister are both intelligent and they are being raised by a great single mom, who tries to give them the best of everything. Michael understands his attempt to be "street-wise" and often gives him advice on being a good person and doing what's right.

"Now run along, so you don't miss that school bus."

D.J. runs off and Michael jumps into his newly elbowed-shined, Porsche Panamera S and exits the parking garage. While on the freeway, his phone rings. His digital display reads "incoming call from Francisco." Michael verbally accepts the call.

"Hey Francisco, what's up man?"

Francisco clears his throat.

"Morning Michael." How far out are you?

"I'm just leaving Downtown", says Michael. "What's up?"

"Hey can I get you to stop off at the next exit and pick up an ink cartridge for my printer?

"Sure you can, but where is that beautiful wife of yours Francisco?" asked Michael. Francisco chuckles.

"She had a class this morning and she's going to be tied up most of the day...but if you can pick that up for me, I surely would appreciate it".

"No problem man, I got you!" Michael puts on his turn signal.

"Ok, thanks. Love you man!"

Michael smiles.

"Love you too bro, see you shortly".

Michael pulls into Office depot and a few minutes later returns, cartridges in tow.

Michael pulls up in front of a beautiful 6000 square foot home, parks his Porsche, and uses his key to enter the home. He closes the door behind him and takes a look around.

"Hey Francisco, it's just me, where are you?"

Francisco is in the kitchen. He responds, then finishes his drink.

"Hey I'm in the kitchen" I'll meet you in my study. Do you need anything while I'm down here?"

Michael heads for the study.

"No, I'm good bro!"

Michael enters the study and takes a seat on the plush sofa. He pulls a folder out of his briefcase and waits for Francisco, who soon enters the room in his motorized wheelchair. Michael is always glad to see him. Not only is he a dear friend, but he helps Michael with his business affairs as his personal accountant. Francisco is paralyzed from the waist down and Michael has always made it a point to see about him, treating him no different, never making him feel pitied or less than. He loves Francisco and would do anything for him. After his accident it was hard to watch his thriving, handsome, Puerto Rican friend adjust to life in a wheelchair, but Michael was right there by his side. Francisco has always admired his character and appreciated his loyal friendship. He would never forget Michaels love and support at one of the most difficult times in his life. They are family.

"Francisco, you normally don't get me out here in the middle of the week unless something is terribly wrong. So I've got to know, are you okay?"

Francisco looks surprised.

"What do you mean? I'm okay Mike. My health is fine. Hey man, I didn't mean to scare you, but I called you out here today to give you some really good news about the restaurant. First of all, your quarterly gross profits for the year are actually better than your yearly gross profits from four years ago by at least 18% … and also, because I knew you would want to talk to Tim …you know…about giving him a raise since he has been working so hard".

Michael was relieved and glad to hear the news. And yes Tim had been working hard to make the restaurant a success and he did. Michael was just waiting for the right time to give him a raise and reward him for his dedication and hard work.

"You're so right about that. I'm so thankful for him and I'll tell him the good news tonight at closing. Francisco, while I'm out here and in no rush, with plenty of time to burn, I can run you to the gym and get a good workout in as well".

Francisco would love to but…

"As much as I would love that, I've got a lot of stuff I need to get done early because the Mrs. has made plans for us tonight."

Michael gives him the 2 thumbs up.

"Well go ahead then man and say no more… And speaking of the Mrs., I think I just heard her pullup." Seconds later, they hear Francisco's wife enter the house. Francisco yells.

"Honey, we're down here in the study."

"Okay, Papi. Is that Michael's car parked out in front of the drive-way?"

"Yes dear, he's here", says Francisco. She enters the study, immediately walks over to Francisco, gives him a big kiss, asks how his day was as she turns around and walks over to hug Michael and give him kiss on the cheek.

"Hey Michael, It's really good to see you today."

Michael smiles and returns the love.

"It's so good to see you too, Arielle !"

And yes, it's Arielle . The same, tall, honey colored beauty who let herself into Michael's apartment and his shower.

About 8 years ago, a year after his hunting accident, when Francisco realized that Arielle was still going to love him and be there for him in spite of his condition, he decided to go out and find someone who could periodically cater to her needs, hoping to make her feel whole again. Francisco loved Arielle more than anything in the world and her happiness was all that cared about. He knew what it would look like to the world, but he accepted his condition and the fact that his wife would be affected in one of the most sensitive areas of her life. Intimacy would still be there, but physically, he could no longer make passionate love like he once could and she didn't deserve that. He made peace with his decision and promised to find someone who could satisfy her physically, make her feel desired and fulfill her sexual needs. It was his gift to her. Even though she fought it in the beginning, Arielle agreed to honor his gift. They set out to find the perfect man to fulfill her sexual desires. Francisco researched the finest, most exclusive escort services for months. It was a bit of trial and error until they finally came across Michael. Arielle was taken aback to find out that among his many jobs, he was also an exclusive, male escort. Francisco who knew, realized…that somehow it made sense. It never crossed his mind, but knowing Michael personal, his upbringing and his love for women, it began to make perfect sense that Michael would be the man for this job.

At first, Arielle and Michael declined as it seemed so wrong, almost like a betrayal to have sex with his best friend's wife. But Francisco pleaded for their support. He made them realize that this wasn't something that was wrong or disgusting. It was his gift to both of them. He trusted Michael with his life and he knew he would make Arielle feel loved, because he knew he loved her anyway. They were all like family and Michael was always there for them. The three of them talked about it for hours and finally Arielle and Michael agreed to honor Francisco's request. Their unique situation began and they never looked backed. Michael, understanding their situation, serviced Arielle in a way that made her feel loved and like the beautiful woman she is.

And now 8 years later, Michael, Francisco and Arielle have formed a friendship bond that's stronger than any family. After all, it was Francisco that actually convinced Michael to invest the monies he earned from being an escort, into opening up the restaurant and the health club. It was the best move Michael ever made. Both the restaurant and health club are very successful. Even though it's been eight years, Arielle still pays every time she and Michael have sex. But those lavender envelopes that ends up in the bottom drawer represent something more than sex. Eight years of not just having sex, but making love has changed the game for Michael...and Arielle ... They both know and the lavender envelopes have become a way of fooling herself into thinking she's not in love with him. Out of love and respect for Francisco, Michael is harboring a secret which he wouldn't dare let out. Somewhere along the way Michael has fallen in love with Arielle . He'd rather take this secret to the grave, than hurt Francisco. So it seems they're just trying to fool themselves; Arielle paying the money all these years, and Michael for not spending it after all this time. Francisco, may be the only one in this triangle that accepts the truth of the matter. But, Francisco is eternally grateful to Michael for not once trying to take the one thing that Francisco loves the most in this world, and that is Arielle .

At the end of the day, there are three selfless people who chose to do whatever it takes in order to make everything work out because they love each other unconditionally. It may not make sense to the world but it's the true meaning of family to them.

After visiting for a little while longer, Michael decides he has to leave. He hugs Francisco and Arielle walks him to his car.

Michael turns to Arielle .

"How is Francisco really doing"?

Arielle takes Michaels hand. She knows he cares.

"He has his good days, and he has his bad days, but the blessing is that the good ones outweigh the bad. He holds a lot from me, not wanting to worry me, but I know he's in a lot of pain, so we just pray every day and keep it moving".

Michael hugs Arielle .

"You know I'm here for the both of you. Just let me handle some of the load."

Arielle takes great comfort in Michael's arms. She closes her eyes and smiles. It's obvious they have a genuine love for Francisco and each other.

"On a lighter note, Francisco has a birthday coming up in a few weeks and I need you to see if you can free up the Saturday before his birthday. I'm throwing a cook out and having everyone over, so check your calendar and let me know if that's good for you."

Michael steps back and heads to his car.

"I will make sure that I'm free that day because I wouldn't miss it for the world!"

"Thank you love!"

Michaels closes his door and drives away. Before he could even make it to the freeway, his cell phone rings and the digital display reads Cheryl.

Chapter Five

The Best Little Whorehouse in Atlanta

"Hey knuckle head".

Cheryl sucks her teeth.

"Whatever. You pea brain! But I didn't call you to make fun of your ugliness. I called to see if you can take a walk-in?"

"When?"

"Dinner time- until" replied Cheryl.

Michael is thinking.

"Is it local and who is it?"

"Yes and its Janet".

Michael thinks.

"Okay, text me the details".

Cheryl is happy.

"Ok, it's on the way bro. Love you man!"

Michael laughs and shakes his head.

"Love you too, and I'll call you tomorrow."

Michael sits back and puts on some Tamia. His plans to catch a movie with his brother were officially cancelled and he was glad he hadn't asked Brandon. His phone beeps and he sees the text from Cheryl which ends with another smart-ass comment. He laughs and turns up the music. Cheryl is Michael's business partner in the escort business, and walk-in is code word for a short notice, fuck date. Cheryl and Michael met for the first time when Michael was fourteen, and she was sixteen, about four years after Michael's parents died in a horrific car accident. This was also around the time Michael and Brandon ran away from their Aunt Sharon, who the courts had appointed as their legal guardian. Although she was next of kin, they had only heard about her from their mother as being her younger sister that was on drugs and mostly living on the streets. Michael often wondered how the courts seemed to overlook the part about drugs and living on the streets.

After four years of neglect and abuse from their Aunt Sharon, Michael took his little brother Brandon and ran away. Uncle O was the only person they knew to run to, but Uncle

O was homeless, living on the streets himself and knew that he could not keep the boys with him. So Uncle O, knowing that his boys needed more than he could give them at the time, took them to his and their father's childhood friend Doris, truth be told, their father almost married Doris before he met their mom. Doris was always a good, loyal friend and she loved Uncle O. Doris is also Cheryl's mother. Cheryl and Michael have always been close since the day they met. Cheryl was slightly overweight and very pretty… and smart. She knew what kind of business Doris ran and as she got older, she helped her mother manage the bookings. Michael and Brandon always treated her like a little sister, even though she was the oldest, and she loved them for that. Her father was not around and some people from the old neighborhood believe Michael's dad was also Cheryl's dad, but Doris has never admitted to it. Doris to take the boys into her home, but under one condition. The boys would have to get their education and make something of themselves. Uncle O and the boys promised that they would. Little did anyone know that

Michael and Brandon would embark on the biggest adventure of their lives…a journey that would change and shape their lives forever. Un-beknownst to the boys, from that day forward, home would be a boarding house within a whorehouse, full of love, laughter, encouragement and family.

With Michael growing up in a whore house, he learned many a things, especially how to please any and all females. This was not a normal upbringing and Michael knew that, but he was thankful that Doris loved him and his brother, even though it wasn't in the most conventional way all the time. Doris encouraged their education and taught them how to cook, clean and be gentlemen. It wasn't long before Michael became intrigued with Doris' business. As a good looking teenager, the ladies were lining up to get a piece of him, and he was knocking them down left and right. They also taught him what women liked in bed. Before long, he became every woman's dream when it came to sex. As he got older, he truly came to respect the sexual desire of a woman and how important it was to make them feel wanted during these encounters.

When it was time for him to go off to college, instead of leaving his younger brother Brandon behind, Michael decided with some help from Uncle O, to go and take back their childhood home from their Aunt Sharon, along with the money from the trust fund he was entitled to now that he was 18. So with help from Uncle O, they went and booted Aunt Sharon out. Michael would raise his brother Brandon, graduate from college and make something of himself just like their mother and father would have wanted for the both of them. Doris was also proud of Michael's determination. By this time, he also realized that he had a talent for satisfying women. So fast forward, Michael and Cheryl started their own escort service that serves them well to this day. Cheryl's only responsibility is managing the business, with Michael being one of their most sought after, exclusive male escorts. Business is booming, money is flowing in and life is just good.

Chapter Six

Wild Horses

It's late October and fall colored trees adorn most of Atlanta. The sun has set and Michael is driving out to an equestrian community, South of Atlanta, where the large homes are on many acres and are at least a mile apart. He pulls up to this four-story mansion with a winding, circular drive-way, gets out of his car and starts walking over to the stables. As he approaches, about fifteen yards away the barn doors swing open and there stands his client Janet. 6 feet tall, red hair, fair skin, approximately size 8 frame with heavy, voluptuous breast, wearing nothing but tan Hermes riding boots. Michael stops in his tracks, amazed at what he is seeing. Janet is one of the most beautiful white woman he has ever been with. Her red hair was glowing in the sun and the backdrop to her body looked as if she was posing in an 18th century painting. Before he could utter words, Janet speaks in her soft raspy voice.

"Take off all your clothes and stay right there."

With no hesitation, he does exactly what she says. Janet disappears back into the stables. It's been five minutes and the anticipation alone has generated Michael's erection. Janet emerges from the stables with two show horses. A black male horse for her and a white female horse for Michael. They mount the horses and head out towards the woods, her in riding boots and Michael naked from head to toe. Janet takes the lead with Michael chasing after her.

Forty-five minutes later they end up in the backyard of her grand mansion. She steps down off of her horse, and slowly takes to the grass, lies on her back with legs wide open, and boots in the air. Michael moves in between her legs, enters and makes love to her like a wild animal. She belts out continuous screams of passion at the top of her lungs. The scene alone is crazy, yet sexy in a country song kind of way. Thrust after thrust, nearby the male horse is up on his two hind legs dancing around, neighing loudly while the female horse is trotting around in a circle, enticing the male horse. The move and smell of hot, steamy, heavy sex is floating in the air. After twenty minutes or so, Michael ejaculates inside of Janet. They both lay on the grass a few minutes longer, watching the horses run and play. For a moment, it feels surreal for Michael, this country scene. A black man in the green grass with his white lover surrounded by black and white wild running horses under orange, yellow, crimson trees. Then got up and walked back to the stables to put the horses away. Still naked, still lusting. Afterwards, they went in the house to shower and later ended up on a silk Isfahan Persian rug in front of the fireplace. The crackling fire is going as Janet feeds Michael cheese, crackers and wine... They spend the next three hours feverishly making love on and off until she falls off to sleep.

Michael quietly eases out, retrieves his clothes and drives home to go to bed. Hours later his 9 am alarm goes off .Michael wakes up, turns it off and drifts back off to sleep.

Chapter Seven

All Man

The phone rings. Michael is startled and reaches for his phone.

"Hello?"

Michael actually looks at the caller ID. It's Cheryl.

"Hey bro, it's me Cheryl. Did I catch you at a bad time?"

Michael yawns.

"No sis, I should've been up. Is everything good?"

"Yea bro, everything is good, but can we meet up for lunch today?"

Michael sits up, he's up now.

"And why not? I've got a few hours before I have to be at the Health Club. So where do you want to meet?"

"Let's do Elements."

"Cool, I need to talk to Tim about that long overdue raise he deserves anyway.

Cheryl chuckles. "I know he will really appreciate that."

"Yes, indeed, I'll see you at the restaurant in about in an hour".

"Ok, cool!"

Michael is exhausted, but that's how the grind goes. He gets up and stretches before heading to the shower. Thirty minutes later enters his restaurant through the back door. The first person he sees is Tim who meets him half way.

"Hey, Michael, Cheryl is in the Fire section waiting for you."

Michael gives him the man hand-to-chest greeting.

"Yeah I know, but you got a minute?"

Tim gives him a look.

"I'm right in the middle of lunch hour, does it look like I got a minute?"

Michael smirks.

"Well you might want to make time to hear what I've got to say."

Tim is interested now.

"Ok dawg! What you got? And you better hurry! You've got two minutes!"

"You know that 10% raise you've been crying about for over a year now?"

"Hell yeah", says Tim.

"Well, why don't we make it 15% and call it even? "And before Michael could get another word out, Tim hugged him so tight and started yelling...

"Thank you, Thank you, Thank you!"... over and over.

Michael was pleased to see Tim so happy. He really deserved this.

"I thought your ass was so busy!"

Tim steps back, still excited, but knows there is a lot to do.

"I am, but you just don't know how happy I am right now. I can finally get my boyfriend a new truck! "

Michael agrees.

"Yeah he really needs to get out of that old beat up truck."

"Michael, I love you man," Tim says as he backs away, fist-pumping the air...

"I love you too brother", said Michael. Then realizing that the situation was getting a little heavy…"Now get in there and earn that 15% raise".

Michael smiles and heads into the restaurant to have lunch with Cheryl, who is seated and scrolling on her phone. He walks up behind Cheryl and kisses her on the back of the neck. Cheryl recognizes the cologne and doesn't even have to turn around.

"Hey Bro!"

Michael takes a seat. It's not often Cheryl summons him to lunch, so he is curious as to what this meeting is really about.

"Ok, what's on your mind Sis and don't say nothing, because I know you well enough by now to know when something is on your mind. So spit it out."

Cheryl gives him a look like she's a little girl with a secret she's dying to tell.

"Ok man, alright! Benny keeps on calling me! I mean like every day, like every day he's calling! He says he will pay anything…like money is no issue anything… just for one night with you."

Michael sits back in disbelief. Like did she really just drag him down here to tell him this bullshit?

"Wait a minute Cheryl. You've known me most of my life and you of all people, should know that I can never be gay. I'm just not built that way. The day that I freely submit to having sex with a man will be the day that I lose my manhood forever. And a man without manhood, is something I just can't understand. My ability to satisfy women is based on my love for women! So Cheryl, don't come at me with that Benny crap anymore, ever! I am taking my manhood to the grave with me."

Cheryl looks somewhat defeated, slightly embarrassed. She knows better and she realizes Michael is serious.

"Ok, alright! I get it!...I'm sorry, you're right. I won't ask again.

Michaels knows she gets it now. He's satisfied and moves on to something else. Its one thing to question his manhood or his genuine love for women...that's does not bode well with him at all. He is all for everyone and their sexual preference, but he himself is not gay and never will be. Michael and Cheryl enjoyed the rest of their lunch together, laughing and talking.

Michael is about to leave and notices Tim zipping pass.

"Hey Tim, do you need me to hang around any longer?"

A busy Tim waves his hand and gestures an "OK"

"After you just giving me a raise? No, I think I can handle it. You go on and do your thing."

Michael took advantage of the rest of the day to finish up some paperwork at the health club. He even managed to get a quick workout in. It's now 7:30 PM, and Michael is back at his high rise loft apartment. He showered and now he's taking a nap. Minutes later, suddenly Michael is startled by the warmth of Arielle 's naked body crawling under the covers with him.

"Arielle ! You almost scared the crap out of me!"

Arielle is somewhat surprised, but can't help but smile.

"Oh, Papi! I'm sorry. What are you doing sleeping? Did you forget we had an appointment?"

"Oh no", replied Michael "Never would I ever forget about you, Princess. I didn't get much sleep last night and I just needed a little nap after working out at the gym, but I'm good now."

Truth be told, Michael is exhausted but may just have received a second wind at the site of this beauty...but it shows that he is tired. Arielle softly kisses Michael on the lips.

"Papi, why don't we just take a nap together?"

"Are you sure?" Michael is always ready, willing and able to make love to Arielle . No amount of exhaustion could keep him from loving her. .

"Absolutely! You're tired and I just want to watch you sleep. I'll wake you in a few hours", she said.

Michael, admiring Arielle 's compassion, kissed her back and laid his head upon her bosomas he fell off to sleep. Arielle caressed his face as she lovingly watched him slowly drift off. She began to think of past times of their love making. She gaped over every inch of his beautiful, brown, sculpted body. In this moment, she realized her love ran deep for Michael.

Chapter Eight

No Words

The clock reads 1:00am. Michael finally opened his eyes again. Smiling wide and deep, feeling rejuvenated and realizing Arielle has left, he retrieves the lavender envelope from under the pillow and puts it in the bottom drawer along with the rest of them. He watches a movie before falling back off to sleep.

Later that day Michael pulls into the parking deck at the bank. He parks and takes the elevator to the 26th floor and walks up to the receptionist.

"I have a noon appointment with the CEO, Mrs. Waters".

The receptionist takes serious notice and she likes the view. Her body language shifts as Michael adjusts his shirt.

"You must be Michael?"

"I am", says Michael.

With a cute little sexy smile and a look of curiosity, the receptionist speaks.

"Sir, you may go in now. She's expecting you."

Michael winks and walks into the office of Mrs. Waters, who is sitting behind a big lavish, black wooden desk on the phone. This is Mrs. Waters, a 41 year old, Brazilian beauty. She looks up just long enough to raise one finger, acknowledging Michael and letting him know that she would be with him soon. Michael stops right in his tracks, without saying a word. It begins. Michael is not allowed to say a word in her presence, that's the rule. Michael stands still and waits for her to finish. He is piercing her soul with his sexy, alluring eye stare…and she can feel it! Moments later she gets up from her desk and walks right pass Michael without saying a word. He turns and follows her to the elevator which is the only one of five that goes down to the basement where the furnace is housed. Once they are on the elevator, Mrs. Waters push the basement button and turns to Michael, leaning in close and whispers.

"Michael you really look handsome today, and you smell so nice and sexy."

She puts her finger over his lip and he nods his head and smiles. As soon as the elevator door opens to the basement, Michael hurries over to get the trash can, like he has done before on many occasions and places it between the elevator doors to keep them from closing. Out of service. Mrs. Waters walk over to a bench, sits down and meticulously pulls her hair up into a ponytail. Michael moves toward her, takes off his shirt then unbuttons his jeans while watching them drop to his feet. Now he is standing there with his hand on his hip, wearing nothing but his jeans which are now covering his feet. He is still... he's not allowed to touch nor allowed to speak. So he just stands there with his penis is hard as a rock, anticipating what is to come next.

Mrs. Waters is married to one of the wealthiest men in town, who happens to be very handsome and will give her anything she wants. She loves the fact that her husband has an average penis, because ever since she was a teenager, she's always been fascinated with

performing oral sex… which she has mastered…
All of her life she's has been on a quest to
find the perfect penis, which is undoubtedly
Michael's. She has to have that perfect penis
once a week. Michael relishes in the fact that
she handles him well, very well.

After staring at him for some time, she
finally takes his cock into her mouth and starts
to suck slowly and passionately, increasing her
thrust for the next 40 minutes. Every time he
comes, she swallows and keeps on going. This
is fellatio at its best. Michael is so weak his
knees buckle after the fourth ejaculation. She
slowly pulls his cock out of her mouth as if she
didn't want to waste not one drop. She stands
up, licks her lips and puts on her lipstick to
return to her normalcy.

After Michael and Mrs. Waters are done,
she moves the trash can away from the elevator
door and takes the elevator back up to her office.
Michael stays behind to get dressed, then he
leaves. It was a good morning. Michael climbs
out the whirlpool and heads to the sauna. Just
as he gets totally relaxed, Amy runs in.

"Michael I got a call in my office that you need to take right away."

Michael sees the on the look of panic on Amy's face. He quickly takes off. What's happening?

"Hey this is Michael!"

Brandon voice is shakey.

"Michael its Bran. It's about Uncle O. Somebody beat him up pretty good and he is in ICU at the hospital... unfortunately they won't let me see him."

"I'm on my way".

Michael quickly gets dressed and heads to the Hospital. When he arrives, he learns Uncle O is still unconscious. Brandon told him that the doctors gave him something to make him go to sleep. Uncle O has four broken ribs, his left arm is broken, and he has a concussion but the doctors say he should be fine in a couple of weeks.

"Fuck!"

Michael in distress, this can't be happening!

"I'm going to need you to stay with him a little bit longer while I run over to the old neighborhood.

"I need to go with you," says Brandon.

"Calm down Bran. I'm just going to peep the situation and I promise, I won't do anything without you, so just stay here and I'll be back to relieve you. Ok?"

Brandon knows he's not going, so no need to ask. He knows what this means.

"Alright."

Michael leaves for an hour or so and then returns to the hospital to check back in on Uncle O. He is a bit anxious, but looks very worried. Brandon needs to know...

"Hey, what did you find out?"

Michael motions him away from Uncle O's bedside.

"Mr. Smith at the liquor store said it was three young G's from a few blocks over"

Brandon gasps.

"Were they Marcus's boys?"

"Mr. Smith didn't think they were, but he was able to give me at least two names and I got some people on it.

Brandon looks alarmed. This doesn't sound good.

"What people?"

"Didn't I tell you I got this?" said Michael.

Brandon relaxes. He glances over at a bandaged and bruised Uncle O sleeping. He knows what this means and he wants it to mean exactly that.

"Yeah I know… but this just pisses me off and all I want to do is hit somebody!" Michael puts his hand on Brandon's shoulder. He is pissed too, but he has to remain calm for Bran. He's definitely going to handle this.

"You got your family that you need to think about. If something happen to you, where would they be? I just need to reach out to Marcus to make sure that he doesn't have to take the heat for my actions."

Brandon agrees.

"Do what you need to do, Bro."

Michael leaves to go pay Marcus, a childhood friend a visit. He's an straight up O.G. that runs the local gang. Marcus is as mean and as bad as you can get. As the streets call him" mean as a mother fucker Marcus". Michael knows he has to warn him about what's going down and he's glad that none of his crew is involved. Either way, Marcus will want to make it right.

It's late and Michael drives into the local projects which is a place that most people stay away from after dark. Everybody on the block are watching, lurking to see "who the hell is this fool driving through in this nice car at this time of night." He pulls up in front of Marcus's building and his car is surrounded by at least ten gang bangers who are visibly strapped. Michael exits his car. One of the gang members get right in Michael's face, outweighing him by at least forty pounds.

"Hey man, what the fuck you want?"

Michael doesn't blink, he knows what it is.

"I need to see Marcus. Tell him it's Lil Mike."

The gang member steps back and looks Michael up and down.

"Hey ya'll, this fool here is Lil Mike!" Other members chime in.

"No shit!"

"Dawg, the OGs talk about you all the time. They say you got a heart like a lion and can fight like a motherfucker. Dude, you like a legend around here. Come on man, we gonna take you to Marcus. You get much respect."

They take him inside. Marcus is engaged in a conversation with two of his top right hand men, when he looks up and sees Michael standing on the other side of the room.

"Well, Well, Well, look at what the fucking wind done blew in here. I thought I told you not to bring yo' ass down here... cause this ain't the place for you Dawg."

Michael takes a deep breath and tilts his head.

"It's good to see you too, Fool!"

Marcus gives him a complete look-over. It's been a minute since he's seen his old friend.

"I ain't saying I'm not glad to see you...but you could've called a brother first."

By this time, Michael has made his way over to Marcus and leans over and whispers...

"Hey it's Uncle O and I need to talk in private".

Marcus concurs.

"Done. Everybody out! Get out now!"

They all leave and Marcus asks, "What's wrong with him?"

Michael went on to explain.

"He got jumped by three thugs in front of Mr. Smith's Liquor store and he's in the hospital. But he's going to be alright.

Marcus asks, "Was it some of my guys?"

"Nah!"

Marcus is cool.

"Then what you doing here? Do you need me to handle it?"

"No" said Michael. "But the way I'm going to handle this situation, it could very well come back on yah."

Marcus is not moved, he could care less about aftermath when it comes to handling situations, especially for family.

"Uncle O is like family to me and I don't give a damn if it does. What you need in order to handle your end? You need gun? You need Goons? Whatever it is you need, I got cha. Just say the word."

Michael expects nothing less from his boy.

"I'm good! I got a buddy that handles a lot of top secret security shit. I'm going to make a statement that puts the fear in these streets.... and Marcus, you got to reap the benefits."

Marcus chuckles, he is really glad to see Michael and pissed off at the same time. He's got to let him handle his business and he's got his back always.

"Cool by me, Michael. But you be careful man …and it's about time you brought your high class ass down here. I was beginning to think you were too good for us!"

Michael laughs.

"Don't forget I can still whoop yo ass!"

Marcus laughs. That's his boy!

"You wish and tell Brandon I those got kicks he asked for."

Michael looks surprised. What does he mean tell Brandon…?

Marcus knows what's up.

"You seem surprised, Michael. Brandon always stays in touch with me. He never forgot where he came from."

Michael gets the dig, but Marcus knows this life ain't him, never really has been.

"Marcus, you know I love you like a brother and I'm always here for you man."

"Yeah, I know", says Marcus. "Now let's get yo candy ass off this side of town before it gets too late."

They hug and laugh it off. Michael heads back to the hospital to relieve Brandon.

The nurse pulls back the curtain half way. As she leaves, Uncle O wakes up to find Michael sleeping in the chair next to his hospital bed.

"Hey Michael! Hey. Hey, wake up!"

Michael wakes. He gets out of the chair and goes over and stands next to Uncle O's bed.

"Hey Unc, how you feeling?

Uncle O moves his neck around. He's still sore.

"I'm feeling good, but I would be feeling a hell of a lot better if I had a short dog."

Michael smiles. He's glad Uncle O is really OK.

"Brandon will be back in a little while and I'll get him to stop at the liquor store and you pick you up one. So, Uncle O, tell me what happened?

"I was coming out of the liquor store when I ran into these three young punks. One of them pushed me and before I could think, I had hit him about two or three times. By then, the other two jumped in the fight. and I tried to stay on my feet, but one of them had some fight training ya' know? After a while, it just went black man and …I couldn't remember anything until now. How long have I been in here?"

"Since yesterday about this time", replied Michael.

Uncle O starts squirming, now he's anxious.

"When they gonna let me out of here?

"Sometime today."

Uncle O is determined.

"Give me a few days and we gonna go get them fools!"

Michael smiles. Uncle O is serious.

"How did I know you was gonna say that! And don't you worry cause I'm on it."

"Good!"

Uncle O takes a deep breath and quickly falls back to sleep. Michael sends a text to Brandon to ask him to stop to pick up Uncle O a short dog. Less than an hour, Brandon walks into the room.

"Hey, you must have been right around the corner."

Brandon sets the bags down and checks on Uncle O.

"I was just getting off the exit when you called and there was a liquor store right there. So, how is Uncle O?"

"He just went back to sleep and he is doing fine. He's tough as nails."

"Bro, what about that other thing? asked Brandon.

You remember my friend Damion? asked Michael.

He remembers.

"Yeah. Is that the guy you introduced me to at Francisco's cookout last year?" "Well Damion has a security firm and they are into some high tech kind of shit. I just got off the phone with Damion and its all going down tonight. Oh, by the way, I spoke with Marcus last night and he told me to tell you he got those kicks you wanted."

Brandon is slightly taken aback. He knows Michael may go in on him.

"Oh yeah? What else did he tell you?

Michael is calm, he is just always concerned about his brother. He doesn't want him to get mixed up with Marcus and his crew.

"He just told me how you guys always stay in touch which I think is a good thing. He has always been like a brother, but I need you to be careful when you're over there. So keep your head on a swivel. There's a lot of bad shit going on over there."

"Yeah, I know." says Brandon.

"By the way, Bran, the Doctor said Uncle O can get out today if he has somewhere to go so that he can get some much needed rest. I think its best that he goes to your house since there is no transit system out where you are."

Brandon agrees. Uncle O really needs to sit still and get some rest. It won't be long before he is back to being Black Rambo out in the streets.

"Yeah, and I agree, so you go and get some rest. I got this."

Michael and Brandon hug and he tells him to tell Uncle O he loves him and he will come over to check on him later and leaves. As he heads to his car, Michael is still pissed off and ready to handle business. Uncle O is his family and no one messes with his family. It's been a while since he had to "go back to the hood", but it's time and he's ready.

Michael is awakened by a text from Damien at 10:38 p.m.: "They're here at Mr. Smith's Liquor Store. Let me know how long will it take you to get here?"

"20 minutes".

Michael pulls up in front of the liquor store and shortly afterwards he looks across the street and makes eye contact with Damien. Damien points to three guys standing at the corner. Michael then nods his head to acknowledge that he sees them. Damien then gets out of his truck and walks towards the liquor store with Michael following closely behind him. They go into the liquor store to have a brief conversation when Damian's alarm goes off on his watch. A sixty second countdown begins. Damien and Michael slowly walk out the store, down the sidewalk toward the corner where the three guys who jumped Uncle O are standing. When the timer on Damien's watch gets to 15 seconds, he yells

"Hey, y'all like to beat up on old man, huh?"

The three guys then turn towards Michael and Damien, and before one of the guys could get out of his mouth, "Who wants to know?,",… a big black SUV pulls up behind them and five huge men exit with their faces covered, leaving only the driver inside only. Only 19 seconds go by until they reenter the SUV and drive away, leaving the three guys on the sidewalk, bloody, unconscious and stripped of their weapons.

Damian turns to Michael and asks, "Is that cool or what?" Michael smiles from ear to ear, pretty much in shock. What the hell just happened?

"Dang, that was some cool straight-gangsta shit!"

They walk back to their vehicles and drive away. Michael woke up around 8:30 a.m. and picked up a newspaper while on his way to Brandon's to check on Uncle O. The headline read: "Three drug dealers beaten within inches of their lives and there are no witnesses or suspects." Michael takes a deep breath. Justice served.

Chapter Nine

Alive Man Walking

It's a beautiful Saturday morning. Michael walks in to Brandon's kitchen and there is Cameron and Brielle watching their mom Chanel cook pancakes and sausage for breakfast. The aroma brought back memories of when they were kids and their mom and dad were still alive. Cameron and Brielle have noticed Michael and come running to give him a hug. He picks them both up and carries them over to where Chanel is standing and gives her a kiss on the cheek.

"Good morning Michael, breakfast will be ready in just a moment. Uncle O and Brandon are in the family room."

Michael walks towards the family room with Cameron over his shoulder and Brielle on his hip, goofing off and having fun. He adores these kids and they love him even more. They make it to where Uncle O is sitting. Michael dumps them down onto the sofa and tickles on them for a while.

"Okay kids, I got to talk to Uncle and your dad for a minute, I'll come find you in a little while and we will play some more."

The kids agree and go running back to the kitchen. Michael smiles at Uncle O and gives the newspaper to him. Uncle O looks at the front page and sees the headline. He smiles and passes the paper to Brandon. Brandon looks at the front page and the three of them look at each other Uncle O proudly speaks.

"Now that's what family does for one another. Michael you did well."

They have breakfast together and spend most of the day just having fun as a family. Before Michael gets ready to leave, he, Chanel and Brandon sit down to have a conversation with Uncle O. Michael starts.

"Uncle O, the three of us have decided that it's time for you to come in off the streets and accept the responsibility of being the head of this family, because this family is not whole without you. We also think it's time you move into our old house. You know Mom and Dad would have wanted that, as well as we do. These kids need to be able to spend more time with you, like Brandon and I did when we were little.

Uncle O fights the tears, but he is emotional.

"Okay, Okay! Stop right there Michael. I get it! I get it! I'm getting too old to be living on the street. I had planned on moving into the old house before the winter, anyway. So say no more, it's done!"

Michael and Brandon couldn't be happier, Chanel was boo-hooing and everybody was hugging each other. Uncle O never felt so loved. This was his family and he wanted nothing more than to be a patriarch. He thought about his old friend and hoped that he was proud. He finally had the family he always wanted and it felt good. Michael was overwhelmed.

"Hey you guys, let's say a prayer."

They all join hands as Michael leads them in prayer. Afterwards it was time for Uncle O to get some rest. Michael told Uncle O that would come by on Monday to take him shopping for some new clothes. Uncle O smiled. He knew

it was time to let his boys take care of him…
after all he was like their father.

"Cool!"

Michael hugs everyone again before having
to leave. When he got to the door his eyes
began to tear and he turned to face the family.

"Hey you guys, I love you all so much and
this is the best day ever…that's all."

Chapter Ten

Don't Judge A Book By Its Cover

On his way home Michael's IPhone watch alarm goes off. It's a reminder that he has a client in town for the weekend who happens to be the ex-wife of a very famous actor. Whenever she's in town Michael visits her hotel suite. Back to the pleasure of business.

Michael makes it home and after showering and changing clothes he heads over to the hotel to meet his client. Upon entering her hotel suite, he looks at her, smiles and she smiles back. She holds up a timer set to go off every hour on the hour, starting now.

Its late afternoon and they start fucking like wild beasts. It's hard, it's hot and it's heavy. At first there is no sound, but the occasional moan, scream and whimpers escape. One hour later the alarm goes off. Michael has to leave the bed until the alarm goes off again in one hour... then they go back to having more, aggressive sex. This continues until 6 o'clock a.m. This is her thing. Call it strange but she can't stand foreplay and she doesn't like to cuddle. Michael calls it anything she wants. She really likes it rough... really, really rough. In between the alarms, they have separate rooms and she sometimes takes a power nap. Michael always leaves at 6 o'clock a.m. She needs to rest all day Sunday before her flight out on Monday. Just like clockwork, she's back in town every 3 weeks to literally repeat the same process. Michael often thought about his encounters with this client... that this process could help some of his other clients lose four to five pounds per session, which coined the term "SPEED FUCKING," a process in which Michael currently uses with eight other clients as a workout routine.

After sleeping most of the day away, Michael is awakened by his phone. It's Arielle .

"Hello Arielle ."

"Hello Michael, sounds like you were asleep," she replies.

Michael sits up. He is glad to hear her voice.

"Yes. I was up all night and I'm just trying to get caught up on some sleep."

Arielle pretty much knows what that means.

"Well, I just called to remind you about Francisco's birthday cookout and the fact that I know how bad you are when it comes down to picking a gift. So, I'm just going to say if a printer for his computer were to magically appear, that is something he can use. Hint, Hint!"

Michael laughs.

"You know me like the back of your hand and I love you for that."

Arielle smiles.

"I love you too Michael. Now get some rest and I will talk to you later."

Michael is up early the next morning and goes by to pick up Uncle O. The first stop is Hideoki Bespoke, an exclusive men's boutique, where Michael drops about three grand on Uncle O. Second stop Macys and he spends another grand or so. The third stop is the barbershop. When Uncle O gets out of the chair and looks at himself in the mirror, it brought tears to his eyes. He felt like a new man. He was clean with a fresh haircut and not to mention he smelled good. He walks over to Michael.

"I had forgotten that he was in there."

Michael is moved. He waited for this very day, when Uncle O would clean up and live and truly be the head of their family as father and grandpa.

"Uncle O, I always knew you would find your way back."

Uncle O is fighting tears.

"I don't know what those guys are going to do out there in those street without me!"

They laugh.

"Trust me, Uncle O. They will make due. Now let's go by the restaurant and blow Tim's mind."

"On one condition", says Uncle O.

And what's that? asked Michael.

"You got to take me by the bank first, so I can get some money to tip the waitresses!"

Michael stops and teases Uncle O.

"Yeah right! And I guess you're going to send me in the bank with a note to give to the teller?"

Uncle O straightens up with a what you talkin' bout Willis look on his face.

"Ha-Ha funny Michael. I got several accounts at the bank, all of which have money in them…money that I'm going to leave to Cameron and Brielle.

Michael stands corrected.

"Does Brandon know about this?" he asks.

"Yeah fool", says Uncle O.

"Uncle O, why are you always crying broke to me?

"So I can spend your money and save my money for the kids. You know you guys are all I got and if your daddy was here he'd want to buy the kids their first car, so I just want to be able to give them that experience."

Michael is touched.

"Uncle O, the best experience you can give them is having a home, like you now have, where they can come and visit whenever they want. Trust me, that's going be fun. Those were some of me and Bran's best memories. When you used to babysit us, we had so much fun."

"Yeah we did, didn't we? Uncle O remembers...

They pull up to the bank and go inside. Uncle O approaches the teller, a very cute 46 year old woman who is a little on the heavy side. Just like Uncle O preferred.

"Hello Betty!"

Even though he's been going through her line for the last 4 years, she doesn't recognize him until he opens his mouth. Her mouth drops open and she is absolutely speechless for at least twenty seconds before she could get a word out.

"O Neal, is that you?"

He responded.

"Yeah Betty, it's me."

Then she immediately picked up the phone and called several coworkers with an emphatic request, while continuing to stare at Uncle O.

"You need to get over here. You won't believe who's at my window."

Within seconds, most of the bank employees are at Betty's workstation. One of the other women mistakenly looks at Michael and asks, "Are you an athlete?

Betty quickly reels her in.

"Not him girl! The other one!"

All eyes are on Uncle O until he asks.

"Ladies. Y'all don't recognize me?"

In unison they all respond, "O'Neill is that you?

Uncle O knows he looks good, but loves the attention.

"Damn, ladies was I that tore up?

Betty blushes.

"No! We just have never seen you clean shaved and all dressed up before and …O'Neill you really look nice."

"Thank you Betty," Uncle O proudly responds. He finished his banking transaction and said goodbye to her and the other ladies, then he and Michael headed out. One of the tellers ask Betty who is the young man with O'Neal

"Girl he is so fine so I am going to have to change my panties… that is one good looking man."

"That's O'Neal's nephew, fine men run in that family," says Betty. The other teller says, "Girl I saw the way you were looking at O'Neil." She winks.

Betty sheepishly smiles.

"You know he has always been kind to me, but I have never looked at him in a physical kind of way until today."

Later, Michael and Uncle O enter the restaurant from the rear door of the kitchen and they walk over to Tim, who looks busy as usual.

"Hey Michael didn't think I would see you today."

Michael can't wait for him to see the surprise.

"Oh, I'll be in and out in a few minutes." Just then, Tim turns to Uncle O and blindly speaks.

"How are you doing sir?

Uncle O replies with a playful attitude, "Who you calling Sir you little shit?" And Tim almost faints when he takes a second look, before asking...

"O'Neal is that really you?"

"Yeah it's me you shit head now get your tail over there and fix me a plate before I go stick my hands all in your pots," scoffs Uncle O.

Tim is happy to see Uncle O all better.

'If you do I'll put my foot so far up your tail you won't be able to sit down for days."

Michael steps in to break up the friendly fire of banter.

"Hey, hey, hey break it up you two lovebirds and try and get along."

Tim goes back into frustrated manager mode.

"It's not me, it's him, I was just trying to tell him how nice he looks and how proud I am of him, and there he goes calling me names …get him out of my kitchen please!"

Michael guides Uncle O to a table before things escalate. Tim and Uncle O have nothing but love between them but they are both stubborn. As they walk towards the dining room area Michael pokes Uncle O.

"Why do you always treat him bad?"

Uncle O slows up, smiles and responds. "Because I love him just like I do you and Brandon …and I promise I'm going to work on being nicer to him or her depending on what mood he or she is in that day."

Michael shakes his head.

"Yeah, he can be a little moody sometimes, but he means well."

Uncle O, breaks away suddenly and goes back to the kitchen and without saying a word just walked over to Tim and gave him a long hug and whispers...

"I love you man."

Tim was so shocked, he couldn't say a word. He followed Uncle O back to the dining room and the three of them had a nice lunch together.

After leaving the restaurant Michael took Uncle O home to get him settled in. When they pulled up to the house, Uncle O was quiet. He thought about his old friend and the good times they shared in this house. He was grateful and vowed to make it work, even if it meant facing his demons head on. He wanted to be the man his family could depend on, especially those kids. Uncle O steps onto the front porch.

"Do I need to get the utilities turned on?"

No Uncle O I had everything turned on this morning and Pop's old truck is in the garage. I keep it tuned up and it has insurance on it and the key is hanging in the kitchen by the fridge. You do remember how to drive don't you?"

Uncle O gives Him a look before responding.

"Two things you need when you live on the street, 1 is a place to put your money such as a bank account and you can't get that without a driver's license. So to answer your question, yes I'm a very good driver. But what am I going to eat later?"

Michael sarcastically replies, "I don't know Mr. I got a bank account and I'm a very good driver, why don't you drive your ass down to the grocery store and load up your refrigerator, you can do that can't you? Since I'm going to pay all the utilities."

Uncle O throws a fake punch and Michael throws one back.

"Yeah nephew I can handle!"

"Uncle O, with all jokes aside, mom and dad would be so happy knowing you are going to be here, and if you need anything you can just call me. I love you man."

"Love you too nephew."

Chapter Eleven

Where Life Ends, it Begins

The moon is bright and the night cool and crisp. Michael drives into a gated community north of Buckhead. He enters into an open garage of a multi-million dollar home and the garage door closes behind him. A prominent businessman lives here. Michael enters the home through the kitchen door and makes his way to the theater room where a 40-something year old, slightly overweight white male named Bart, the owner sits watching a pornographic film.

"Hey Bart, what's happening?"

Bart never takes his eyes off the film.

"Not a lot Michael how are you?"

"I'm doing fine," said Michael.

"Good! Michael, Anna is in the bedroom she's getting ready for you, you go up and I'll check in on you in a bit."

Michael turns and heads up to the bedroom. He opens the door and lying on the bed in the nude is Anna, a beautiful white female in her late 20's with a body like a fitness instructor. In her hands is a 12 inch dildo inserted inside her, having a real good time. Michael quickly gets undressed and crawls into the bed. He straddles her chest and places his penis in her mouth. Seconds later she begins having multiple orgasms that goes on for a while. Suddenly the door opens and Bart walks in. He goes in the closet and gets something, then leaves the room without saying a word. Michael and Anna continue and do not give pause at all... An hour and a half later, Michael and Anna are still going strong when Bart enters the room again. He takes a seat in the chair next to the bed. Anna is straddling Michael on her knees and jumping up and down on his big long dark dick. She's looking over at Bart and he has his dick in his hand stroking it. Within minutes everybody is coming. Anna is so exhausted she rolls over and lays down next to Michael, gives him a kiss and thanks him. Michael then gets up and takes a quick shower in the nearby bathroom

On his way out Anna is asleep, and Bart is right next to her in the bed

Michael salutes Bart.

"See you next time."

Bart returns the gesture.

"Thanks man, lock up on your way out."

"Will do", says Michael.

Michael walks into his health spa. He waves as he passes the 10:00 spin class. He heads straight into Amy's office where she is on her computer. Michael gets excited.

"Good morning Amy!" Before she can get a word out, in an exciting voice Michael says, "Amy guess what!"

Amy, not so excited.

What is it?

"Uncle O moved into our old house." Michael does the running man.

"No shit", says Amy. She finally gets excited.

"I shit you not, it was the best day of my life."

"Hey on my next day off, I think I'll go by there and help him decorate."

"Amy he would love that too, you know he acts like he is your daddy." Amy smiles. She is very fond of Uncle O.

"Yeah, O and I have always been cool, so I will go by and make sure he is alright, that will be fun. Do I need to take him shopping?

"That's a no, I already did that, and don't let him fool you into thinking that he is broke! He's got plenty of money. But, if you have to buy anything for the house just put it on the company card."

"Cool Beans!"

Michael leaves out and decides get in a good workout and then heads out for the day. On his way out he sees a missed a call from Francisco, so he calls him back. Francisco picks up on the first ring.

"Hello Michael, how are you doing my friend?

Michael tosses his gym bag and gets into his car.

"I'm doing fine Francisco, what about you?"

"I feel good today", replied Francisco, "but I need to see you as soon as you can get a minute."

"Sure Francisco, I can come by right now, is that okay with you?

"Actually that would be perfect, Arielle has a class and won't be home for a few hours."

"Cool," said Michael. "I'm on my way."

Twenty minutes later Michael pulls up and goes inside. He is calling out to Francisco on his way towards Francisco's office but when he gets there nobody is there. He goes up to the bedroom and there is Francisco lying in bed, which was very unusual for Francisco during that time of day. Michael immediately senses that something is wrong. Francisco didn't even know Michael was in the room until Michael walked over and sat on the edge of the bed. He slowly moves about.

"Hey Michael, I didn't hear you come in, but I need you to just listen. I wanted to tell you this the last time you were here but Arielle came home early, so just let me get everything out before you say anything okay?

Michael is puzzled. He knows something is not right. He nods in agreement.

"Ok."

"Three weeks ago I went to the doctor to have him look at a sore on my left leg and they ran some tests and its cancer. Last Tuesday, I went back to confirm and the cancer has spread throughout my lower body and some of my organs. The doctor said I got a few months at best and he suggests that I get my affairs in order."

Michael is in shock.

"Wait, wait, wait a minute! You mean there is nothing that can be done? People live through cancer all the time, there has got to be something we can do!"

Francisco knows this is going to be hard for Michael. He is trying to be strong for the both of them...the three of them. He has accepted his fate and just wants to get his affairs in order. He knew this day would come, just not this soon. But he is prepared.

"Michael my cancer is being treated by my doctor, he gives me medicine to relieve the pain and it keeps me comfortable. Michael, I am at peace with the whole situation I have had 9 marvelous years since my accident and I owe it all to you Michael."

Michael blurts out, "Francisco you owe me nothing!"

"Oh but I owe you everything. You see Michael, anyone else would have taken advantage of my situation, taken my beautiful wife away from me by now…and that would have killed me a long time ago, but all these years you have neglected your own feelings for Arielle …and I know you have feelings for her, because you have loved us from the beginning and I expected that. I actually wanted that for her and you. If only she knew how much you love her it would have been so easy for her to want to start a life with you, and have children for you… she has always wanted to have children. I hear her crying sometimes late at night and I know that it is one of the reasons why. Michael I know Arielle really loves me and as long as I'm alive she would want to be here for me, but God has made the choice for me to be able to set her free and go on to live a long and happy fulfilling life, one where she will be free to do anything her heart desires while she is still young enough to enjoy it. Michael, I don't want her to mourn over me while I am alive and I know you will be there for her. So Michael, promise me you will help her understand after I am gone. And Michael I truly have nothing but love for you... my friend."

Tears ran down Michael's face. He watches as Francisco smiles, then turns his head away. Michael sees the tears. He knows how hard this must be for Francisco and how he is going to be strong...for everyone, because that is the selfless person he is. Without saying a word Michael stands up, turns and just walks out. Seconds later he drives off. He only makes it two blocks before having to pull over on side of the road where he sat in his car and cried for an hour as the whole world just went by, trying to understand what had just happened and why it happened to someone so deserving. Francisco has been so much more than a friend, he has been Michael's mentor and one might even say he's been the big brother Michael never had. Michael makes it home and literally shuts down for 2 days and begins mourning his friend, so that when the time comes he can be there for Arielle . Having to keep Francisco's cancer from her surely was going to be one of the hardest things Michael has ever had to do besides letting Francisco go.

Three days go by. It's the Thursday before Francisco's birthday cookout and Michael has a dinner engagement with another beauty. A 61 year old, 6 foot tall, size 5, dark chocolate, very sophisticated woman named Vanessa. Vanessa is by far Michael's favorite client that he would actually service for free simply because she is so sexy and so full of class and style. Regal would best describe her. Four years ago her husband passed away and left her a small fortune and she really likes to spend it on Michael. At least three times a year they go out of the country just to shop. She says he reminds her of her late husband whom she loved so dearly and he was quite handsome. But the real reason Michael likes spending time with her is that the pussy is like no other. They go out to dinner at the finest restaurants in the world. They always engage in interesting conversations while fine dining and the conversations always get a little more intimate in the car on the way back home to Vanessa's house. Tonight is no different and by the time they pull into her garage her apple sized breast with nipples the size of grapes are standing at attention. Her dress is wet because she doesn't have on any panties. And all the stimulating conversation and subtle touches has caused her pussy to get really wet. They make their way into the house from the garage, kissing and undressing each other the entire time. They finally get to the downstairs bedroom and she pushes Michael down onto the bed and straddles him on her knees. Immediately she inserts his penis inside her and begins to ride it slow and easy just like Michael likes it. When he is with her, he goes weak with passion and sometimes he comes quickly. Because she doesn't want him coming too fast she quickly puts it in her mouth until it's hard again and climbs right back on top of him and rides it some more. Vanessa is very slow to come and when she finally does come it's like a symphony…and she is quite the noisy one. Hours go by and Vanessa's neighbor is out walking his dog when he hears a loud passionate scream coming from Vanessa's house, screams that the neighbors had become accustomed to hearing over the years so he just smiles and keeps on walking. They finish their dance and shortly afterwards, Michael backs out of the garage and drives away feeling real good, a euphoric high. It's always good with Vanessa... However, the feeling is short lived and before he can make it back to the freeway, sadness sets in and h can't help but think about Francisco's illness, which suddenly brings him to tears. It would be the first of many sleepless nights.

The sun beams in and wakes Michael. He rolls over and picks up his phone to text Francisco.

What time does Arielle go to class?

Francisco replies, "She normally leaves around 9 o'clock a.m."

"Good I'll be there shortly after, and every day thereafter so I'll see you in a little bit."

And just like clockwork 9 o'clock a.m. comes around and Arielle goes into the study with a tray of food.

"Papi, I made you breakfast but I have to go now, I'm on my way to class. "Arielle kisses him and they both say their I love you's and she leaves for school. Michael is parked around the corner and he sees her drive away. He waits until she is out of sight then he makes his way to the house, parks in the driveway and goes inside.

"Francisco it's me, where are you?"

"I'm in my study", answers Francisco.

Michael walks into the room where Francisco is and without saying a single word he hugs him for a long time. Neither of them speak. It was almost as if they had agreed in some secret way, or simply understood never to speak of Francisco's illness again. Michael eventually pulls away.

"Ok Francisco, are you feeling strong enough to get out for a little while today?"

Francisco lights up.

"Sure why not! What do you have in mind? You know it's been months since we took the boat out; let's make it a day on the water."

Francisco gives him the thumbs up. They get him dressed and call down to the dock to have Francisco's boat put in the water. It's a cool spring morning, they arrive at the lake and there are people everywhere. Michael starts to lift him out of the Range Rover, but Francisco wanted to just sit there for a minute to enjoy the view at that moment.

"It moments like this with Arielle that I'm going to miss the most. She loves this lake and being on the water. Michael, you make sure that this is always available to her."

Michael starts to lift him again.

"Got it, now let's go out on the water and have some fun."

And so they did. They spent the day laughing, talking, fishing, even singing while enjoying the view. There was beauty all around and they enjoyed one another's company immensely. A few hours later Francisco's phone rings. It's Arielle .

"Hey honey!"

A frantic Arielle answers.

"Papi where are you?"

"Honey I'm at the lake. Michael came by and we decided it would be a good day for the lake."

Arielle is somewhat relieved.

"You probably should have left me a note or text me to let me know where you were going."

Francisco feels bad. He hates it when Arielle feels afraid and he could hear it in her voice.

"I'm sorry honey but we were having so much fun... but I'll be home shortly okay?

"Ok Papi! Take your time and tell Michael I said hello."

Francisco feels better now that Arielle is at ease.

"Okay honey! I'll tell him. See you soon. Bye now!"

The sun starts to fade and Francisco is getting a bit tired so he and Michael finish up and head back to Francisco's house. Michael drops him off and gets a hug from Arielle before heading by the restaurant for a while. He has a meeting with a client later, but his heart is really not in it to go. Michael decides to call Cheryl and get someone to fill in for him. Cheryl instantly senses something may be wrong with Michael.

"Hey bro is everything okay?"

Michael takes a moment. Things really aren't Ok.

"Yes...everything is okay. I'm just a little tired. It's been back-to-back work and Francisco and I spent the day out at the lake. I just need to rest tonight, but tomorrow I'll be fine."

Cheryl is not totally convinced, but decides not to push the issue. She knows Michael. If there is something going on, she will eventually find out.

"Alright bro I got you."

Michael hangs up and calls Arielle .

She answers right away.

"Hello Michael how are you?"

Michael smiles. Hearing her voice makes things a little easier.

"Everything's good I just called to see if you had cooked dinner yet."

"No not yet. Francisco is taking a nap. He was really tired when he got home. He said you guys had so much fun. I thank you Michael for getting him out the house today."

This is good news. Michael wants his friend to be happy, even if he can't be well. Although he is sad for both Francisco and Arielle , he wants to spend as much quality time as he can, making them both happy. Their bond runs deep and sometimes Michael can't even fathom like without them.

"No need to thank me it was my pleasure. You know I don't spend as much time with him

as I should, but all that is going to change…
and as a matter of fact that's why I was calling.
I was thinking since I'm at the restaurant now,
I can grab some food and come by for dinner
if that's okay with you."

Arielle is pleased.

"Michael, Francisco and I would love it and
make sure you bring some of that pound cake
and those good ol' collard greens.

They both laugh.

"Don't worry I'm going to hook you up, I
will see you in an hour."

Michaels has his chef put together a fine
spread. He heads over and spends a nice evening
with Arielle and Francisco. Eleven o'clock
comes around and they are still having so
much fun, but Michael notices that Francisco
is getting a bit tired. He makes an excuse for
having to leave, so as not to alarm Arielle. They
end the night and he leaves. Another long,
tearful drive home to another sleepless night.

Chapter Twelve

Is This Love

Its two days prior to Francisco's birthday cookout. Michael is awakened from a two hour, deep sleep by his alarm. He hits the snooze button at least twice before he finally gets up to shower, get dressed and off to the airport he. He has to be in New York this afternoon because one of his clients, Kayla, is being awarded at a huge banquet and she wants him to be her date. He decides to do it because he feels it is the least he can do… but of course after the banquet its back to business as usual. They take the subway back to Kayla's building. Kayla is a real estate mogul and she literally owns the building, all 15 floors of this lavish apartment building where she occupies the entire eighth floor. What makes it real sexy is that she's only 27 and a stunning Blasian beauty. Her mother is Asian and her father is black. She can have any man she wants but she is too busy making money. She makes it a point to get some of Michael at least once a week, whether she goes to Atlanta or he flies up to New York... but she really loves playing basketball in the nude at his place. Michael really enjoys her company and greatly appreciates that she is an ex-ballerina. They have sex in some of the most awesome positions and Kayla can go all night long.

Kayla and Michael finally make it to her apartment after flirting and touching and kissing along the way. As soon as they step into the apartment she backs up against the door pulls him to her. She begins kissing, all the while pulling up her dress exposing nudity all the way down to her five inch heels. She undoes his belt and drops his pants and underwear to the floor. Michael is erect and about ready to explode. She takes her right leg and places it on his left shoulder, while her left foot is still on the floor. Then she takes his cock and puts it inside her, and for the next 7 minutes she maintains the position while he aggressively fucks her. She is screaming in ecstasy and her pussy begins to tighten up and throb repeatedly. Michael senses that she is getting ready to have an orgasm so he speeds up and let's go, and they simultaneously climax together. Afterwards he lifts her up and carries her to the bedroom where they continue having sex until he emerges from the apartment four hours later and heads to the airport.

Michael wakes up the next morning around 10 o'clock and he spends the better part of the day just calling family and friends, reminding them of the cookout and making sure that they are all going to be there. Later that evening he meets Brandon, Chanel, and the kids at the restaurant for dinner and of course Uncle O. It's their one Thursday out of the month where they have family dinner. During the night, Michael and Brandon spoke privately and he told him about what's going on with Francisco. Brandon and Cheryl are the only other people that know Michael is servicing Arielle . Brandon and Francisco are also really close so he wanted to give Brandon the opportunity to spend some time with Francisco. He felt as if he owed it to the both of them. Brandon became very emotional and cried after hearing the news. He was thankful and grateful to Michael for letting him know and vowed to spend as much time as possible with Francisco. Hopefully he could be discreet with his feelings. Brandon pulled himself back together as best he could and they made their way back to the family and had a really nice family dinner before heading home for the night.

Typically Michael would go home on a night like tonight to get a good night's sleep and rest up for the next day. But, on this particular night he had the urge to call Arielle to see if she wanted to come by his place for a rain check from their last encounter when he ended up falling asleep on her. Michael stops and picks up her favorite Italian dish and hurries home. Michael quickly sets the table and lights some candles to set the mood. He dims the lights, and he suddenly realizes that he forgot to chill a bottle of Arielle's favorite wine. He walks over to the pantry, looks down to the bottom shelf and breathes a sigh of relief after spotting a whole case of Boones Farm. When she and Francisco were young and couldn't afford much, every celebration began with a toast of Boones Farm, and even to this day Arielle serves the expensive liquor to her guest while she sneaks a drink of the inexpensive Boones Farm. Michael takes a bottle and puts it on ice. He's anticipating a long, good night, so he goes ahead and puts two more bottles in the refrigerator. A few minutes later, a beautiful Arielle steps out of the elevator. It amazes Michael how beautiful she really is and his heart melts. He comes out of the kitchen, where he was warming up the food.

"Hey, how did you get here so fast?"

Arielle gives him a sensual look.

"I can show you better than I can tell you."

Arielle then asks Michael to have a seat on the couch. She stands about four feet away from him and she unbuttons her coat and drops it to the floor. As she stands in front of him, she lets him know that she has already skipped step one by not getting dressed. Michael cannot deny his feelings or his manhood. He loves this woman.

"Does Francisco know that you left the house like this?"

Arielle bends down.

"Yes, he actually encouraged it, which I thought was a little odd."

"Odd or not, I sure do thank him for this."

Arielle gets on her knees in between Michael's legs and starts to undo his pants. Michael remembers his surprise.

"Wait, wait, wait a minute!"

Arielle is puzzled.

"What's wrong? You don't want this?"

Michael slowly moves away and heads for the kitchen.

"Of course I want this! But I made dinner for you, and we should eat before it gets cold".

Arielle , stark naked, walks over to the dining room and there is her favorite meal and her favorite wine. Seeing it almost brings tears to her eyes, she was speechless. Michael walks over and pulls out her chair and she sits down. Michael then slowly gets undressed, all the way down to his socks.

"I was feeling a little overdressed", he whispers. .

Arielle smiled as she took a deep breath. She looked at Michael and realized how much she really loved him. It was more than a sexual attraction, she loved who he was as a person.

"You smell so good, just like fresh flowers."

Michael reached over to pour Arielle a glass of wine and her arm brushed against his leg, and instantly his dick got so hard. He went to the refrigerator and got himself a beer and poured it in a glass. -. Arielle took two sips from her wineglass, got up from the table and walked over to Michael as he pushed away from the table. She straddled him, climbed on top of him and slowly came down on his hard dick. They kissed for what seemed like an hour and after feeling the throbbing of her pussy on his dick, he came inside of her only. Michael lifts her up and carries her to his bed, where they made love over and over again throughout the night, until they both fell asleep. Michael wakes up the next morning and Arielle is still in his arms. He checks his watch, its 7:15 am. Arielle feels that he is awake so she turns over and gives him a kiss.

"Arielle you should hurry and check on Francisco."

Arielle smiles and kisses him again.

"Michael, Francisco will be fine! He wanted me to spend the night here. I don't know why, but he has been acting a little different lately, everything is fine though."

Michael was hesitant at first, but he thought about what Francisco said about making Arielle happy and how much that meant to him. They made love again, then showered together and Arielle left. Michael sat there in heavy thought for a while, realizing exactly what Francisco was doing. He understood where he was coming from, but it felt different now. For years he was content with holding his love deep inside for Arielle and it never bothered him. Now Francisco wanted him to realize his love for Arielle and be with her after he is gone. It was hard to think about it now with Francisco dying. But is this what he had been waiting for? A true love? Could he have a life with Arielle? Children, a family? It was too much to think about right now. The thought of his friend dying put a heavy burden on his heart. Michael goes back to sleep. And when he wakes around 9 o'clock, he calls Arielle to see what she needs him to do for the cookout.

"Michael how are you?"

"I'm good beautiful woman, what time do you need me there today?

"If you can get here around noon that would be great and maybe you can keep Francisco from worrying the caterer and the grill chef."

Michael is amused.

"Say no more, I'll be there shortly."

"Thank you Michael I love you", says Arielle.

Michael feels the same way.

"I love you too!"

Michael gets dressed and goes over to the house and not a minute too soon. Michael gets there and finds Francisco.

"Hey Francisco! Happy Pre-Birthday man!"

Francisco is glad to see him.

"Hey Michael, how are you doing man?

Michael gives him a hug.

"I'm doing fine, but it looks like you are stressing a little bit brother sooo... why don't you just relax and let me take care of everything from here and you just go and get yourself dressed for the cookout."

Francisco takes a deep breath.

"Yeah Michael I wish it was that easy."

Michael sensing a little frustration tries to lighten the mood.

"Trust me, Francisco it is just that easy, today is a beautiful day…and by the way did I say Happy Birthday my brother?"

Francisco concurs.

"Thank you Michael, and you're right it is quite a beautiful day."

Michael continues his dose of positivity and sarcasm

"Today is the first day of the rest of your life. God has blessed us with a beautiful day, so let's just enjoy it, for we will never see this day again. And I guarantee you that nobody will notice if the potato salad doesn't have onions, that the DJ doesn't have a particular song and everybody's gonna have a great time. We're going to celebrate your birthday as if it's your last and God forbid it's not. I love you man, now get your butt upstairs and get dressed. I got this!"

Francisco gives up. Michael is right. He high-fives Michael and takes off to get dressed. 3 o'clock rolls around and people are everywhere and everything is fantastic… the weather is nice and the food is delicious and the music is banging. Francisco strategically makes his way around the cookout taking time out to have lengthy conversations with almost everyone there, telling them how much he appreciates their friendship and how good it is to see them. Meanwhile Arielle has a table full of hot "hunnies," all of which are checking out Michael and wanting to know who that hunk of a man is. Arielle plays it off and says that "it's just Michael and he's a good friend of the family. Francisco and I have known Michael for more than 10 years now."

"Arielle!" says Maria in her heavy Puerto Rican accent, "Let me get this straight. You mean you've known this good looking man for 10 years and not once did you think to introduce him to one of your girlfriends? And you know I've been looking for a man like this all my life."

The ladies laugh and look to Arielle for an answer. Arielle is actually flattered and she sneaks a look at Michael, before lying to the them with a straight face.

"Girl Michael, he's nothing but a player, there's no way I would introduce him to any of my girlfriends."

Maria smirks.

"Player or not girl he would make a great fuck buddy... hell, I would even pay for it" They all laughed.

"Girlfriend you must be loco", replied Arielle .

Eventually she calls Michael over and introduces him to the girls and they all laughed and flirted, playing around getting to know one another. After Michael left the table one of the girls whispered to Arielle .

"He really is a nice guy and I understand why you haven't brought him around...girl that man is really into you. I mean it's so obvious how much he likes you."

"I doubt that very seriously," Arielle tries to laughs it off. "He and Francisco are best of friends. Michael has always been overly protective of me because of that."

They don't buy it.

"Overly protective my ass," belts out Maria. "Girl that man would do you in a heartbeat; I can see it in his eyes."

Arielle tries her best not to look guilty. She knows exactly what they are talking about and part of her wishes that it could be completely a reality. She loved Francisco, but she loved Michael too and she couldn't help the way she felt.

"Enough about Michael, let's just get back to drinking and having a good time."

They did just that and before they knew it darkness had fallen and the crowd started to thin out. Arielle makes sure anyone who had had too much to drink were driven home safely in one of the three limos she rented.

Michael, along with Brandon and his family, stayed behind to make sure everything was done, even though they really wanted to sit and just spend some quiet time with Arielle and Francisco. They knew how much spending time with the kids meant to Francisco. The next hour or so was spent doing exactly what families do; laughing, joking and playing around. Late in the evening, they said their goodbyes and called it a night. Michael makes it home after a great day. He thanks God for his family and prays for Francisco and Arielle . He also prays for clarity and his feelings for Arielle . He just wants to do the right thing by both of them. Finally he showers and once he lays down he immediately falls asleep.

Chapter Thirteen

Selfishly Selfless

Michael is startled by his phone He leans over and sees that its 3:17 am and Arielle is calling. He picks up and before he could say anything he hears Arielle in the background crying hysterically. He jumps up.

"What's wrong? Arielle , what is it?"

Arielle pauses and finally gets to the point where she can speak.

"Michael shortly after you left, Francisco got really sick, and I had to call an ambulance to bring us to the hospital. And Michael, it's really bad!"

She pauses a moment and Michael hears "it's cancer and the Doctor says he has to stay here."

Michael starts to panic.

"Arielle , I'm on my way, just relax, calm down. I'm on my way."

Arielle thanks Michael and they hung up Thirty minutes later Michael is walking down the hospital hallway. Arielle sees him, runs into his arms and cries.

"The Doctor says he has cancer. Francisco is in intensive care and they say he may not make it. Say it's not so Michael, say it's not so."

Michael's heart breaks. This is it, this may be the end for Francisco and Arielle and this is heavy. Michael needs to be transparent.

"Arielle , he does have cancer, but everything is going to be OK. Come, let's have a seat, we need to talk."

He takes her by the hand and they walk across the hall into a vacant room. They sit on the bed and while holding her hands, he looks into her eyes and speaks from the heart.

"Arielle , Francisco has been sick for a while now. He didn't want you to know. He only told me recently, but he's going to be Ok. How much longer he has to live? We don't know that just yet. I'm so sorry.

Arielle doesn't understand. He knew?

"Michael, you knew?

"Yes, but he made me promise not to tell you. We need to be strong for him because he's going through a lot right now"

A few moments later, the Doctor comes into the room and addresses Arielle.

"Mrs. Navarro, Francisco is being moved to a private room and the nurse will give you the details. I will come by first thing in the morning to check on him. His vitals are normal and there's nothing more I can do for him tonight."

The doctor turns to Michael.

"And you must be Michael."

"Yes I am," replied Michael, "and how did you know?"

"Francisco and I have had numerous conversations about your responsibilities as one of his care givers. It's a pleasure to finally meet you."

"Likewise."

They shook hands and the Doctor left the room. The nurse walked up with the directions to Francisco's room. Upon entering Francisco's room, Arielle notices all of the tubes and monitors hooked up to him and almost faints.

Michael helps her to the side of the bed, so that she could touch him and make sure he was still alive. Arielle leans over to place her head on Francisco's chest to say a prayer. She tells him how much she loves him, while Michael holds onto her hand telling her that everything is going to be alright.

Two days pass and Arielle and Michael haven't left Francisco's side. Francisco finally opens his eyes. He looks over to find Michael, sitting up on the sofa asleep. Arielle is lying next to him asleep, with her feet in his lap. Francisco watches them for a few minutes. It makes him happy to see the two most important people to him, together. He knows they will be alright and he knows that they will find a way to be together. He looks towards the ceiling and smiles as his eyes close slowly.

THE END

www.ingramcontent.com/pod-product-compliance
Lightning Source LLC
Chambersburg PA
CBHW031834170626
46807CB00004B/1455